PUFFIN BOOKS

DANNY FOX

Danny Fox wore a beautiful red coat and beautiful thick red clothes, and he was the handsomest and cleverest fox that ever lived. His home was in a cave with Doxie his wife and his three children, Lick, Chew and Swallow.

As you can see from their names, Danny's family were always hungry, and that was why he was on bad terms with the handsome young fisherman whose fish he stole, and why he was marooned on an island by an eagle. But of course a fox like Danny would find a way out of such troubles.

Danny had a heart as well as brains, and when he knew that the beautiful princess loved his enemy the fisherman, and was not allowed to marry him, Danny said he could arrange it. He used all his most cunning tricks, and was the proudest fox in the world when he came safely home from his adventures with all the food his family could want.

Danny's exploits, which the author based on old folk-stories, make sparkling funny reading and he is bound to be a favourite animal character.

David Thomson was born in Quetta in 1914, and spent much of his childhood in a Derbyshire village and on the Moray Firth in Scotland. As a BBC producer, he made many folklore programmes and also did documentary work in Lapland and for UNESCO in Liberia and Turkey.

Other books by David Thomson

DANNY FOX MEETS A STRANGER
DANNY FOX AT THE PALACE

Illustrated by Gunvor Edwards

Danny Fox

David Thomson

Puffin Books

PUFFIN BOOKS

Published by the Penguin Group
Penguin Books Ltd, 27 Wrights Lane, London w8 5tz, England
Viking Penguin, a division of Penguin Books USA Inc.
375 Hudson Street, New York, New York 10014, USA
Penguin Books Australia Ltd, Ringwood, Victoria, Australia
Penguin Books Canada Ltd, 2801 John Street, Markham, Ontario, Canada l3r 1b4
Penguin Books (NZ) Ltd, 182–190 Wairau Road, Auckland 10, New Zealand

Penguin Books Ltd, Registered Offices: Harmondsworth, Middlesex, England

First published 1966
20

Printed in England by Clays Ltd, St Ives plc
Set in Monotype Bembo

To Timothy, Luke and Benjamin

Contents

Contents

1. Danny Fox Steals Some Fish

Danny Fox lived in a small cave on the side of a mountain near the sea. He had a wife called Doxie and three children who were always hungry. Danny and Doxie were often hungry too. The names of their children were Lick, Chew, and Swallow.

Out on the mountain it was very cold, but in the cave it was warm and snug and Danny Fox liked to sleep curled up, with his nose tucked under his hind leg and his long bushy tail round his face like a scarf. Mrs Doxie Fox liked to sleep curled up, with her nose tucked underneath Lick's chin and her front legs hugging Chew and her hind legs hugging Swallow. And Lick, Chew, and Swallow liked to sleep curled up like furry balls against their mother's tummy, while she covered their backs with her long bushy tail like a scarf.

One day the little foxes woke up early and began to whine and yelp and howl.

'Why are you whining, Lick?' said Mrs Doxie Fox.

'I'm whining because I have nothing to lick,' said Lick to his mother, Mrs Doxie Fox.

'Why are you yelping, Chew?' said Mrs Doxie Fox.

'I'm yelping because I have nothing to chew,' said Chew to his mother.

'Why are you howling, Swallow?' said Mrs Doxie Fox.

'I'm howling because I have nothing to swallow,' said Swallow.

'Oh please stop whining and yelping and howling,' said Mrs Doxie Fox, 'and I'll ask your father to fetch some food. Wake up, Danny Fox. It is time to go hunting.'

'I'm not awake yet,' said Danny Fox, and his voice sounded muffled underneath his bushy tail.

'Then how did you hear what I said?' said Mrs Doxie Fox.

'I heard you in my sleep,' said Danny Fox. 'And now I'm talking in my sleep.' But he opened one eye and they knew he was only pretending. Lick, Chew, and Swallow thought he wasn't going to move, so they began their hullabaloo again.

'Oh please fetch some food,' said Mrs Doxie Fox.

'Lick, Chew, and Swallow need something to lick, chew and swallow, and I need something too.'

Danny Fox sat up and yawned. He stretched out his front legs and yawned and he stretched out his hind legs and yawned. Then he put his nose outside the cave and sniffed the cold air.

'Sniff, sniff. I can sniff a rabbit.' He began to run faster and faster up the mountainside, sniffing the ground. Then he saw the rabbit, and yelped and ran faster than ever.

But the rabbit escaped by diving into a crack between two rocks. The crack was too narrow for Danny.

He trotted along and he trotted along. Then suddenly he stood quite still, with his bushy tail stretched out behind him and his long, smooth nose stretched out in front.

'Sniff, sniff. I can sniff a pigeon.' He looked and he looked and he saw a wood-pigeon just below him on the hill, pecking at the ground. He walked very quietly, one step at a time. Then suddenly he sprang at the pigeon. But the pigeon saw him just in time and flew away, and Danny turned head over heels and rolled down the hill.

'Sniff, sniff,' said Danny at the bottom of the hill. 'I can sniff a mouse.' But the mouse ran into its hole.

He trotted along and he trotted along till he came to a farm at the foot of the mountain.

'Sniff, sniff. I can sniff a hen.' But the hen saw him and flew up to a branch of a tree.

'Sniff, sniff. I can sniff a duck.' But the duck waddled into the farmer's house, where Danny was afraid to go.

'Sniff, sniff. I can sniff a goose.' But the goose made such a noise that the farmer came out to see what was

wrong and Danny had to hide beneath a bush. 'I am un-
lucky this morning,' he said to himself. 'What can I find
to take home?'

When the farmer had gone, he sneaked out of the farm-
yard and began to trot along the road. The road went
along by the sea-shore, from the harbour to the town.

'Sniff, sniff. That's funny. I can sniff a fish.'

Danny trotted along and he trotted along, feeling very
hungry. The smell of fish got stronger and stronger, and
the more he smelt it the hungrier he grew. His mouth
watered, his pink tongue hung out and saliva dribbled
from it on to the road. He sniffed and sniffed and began
to run fast. Then he came round a corner and suddenly
stopped.

He saw a horse and cart in front of him. The horse
was walking very slowly, the driver seemed to be asleep
and the cart was loaded with boxes of fish, all gleaming
silver.

Danny Fox walked very quietly, one step at a time.
Then he ran very quietly with his bushy tail stretched
out behind him and his long smooth nose pointing up
towards the cart. When he was near enough he sprang
on to the cart and grabbed a fish from one of the open
boxes. The driver did not look round. Danny Fox lay
down very quietly, hoping not to wake him. His plan
was to eat one fish, then pick up as many as he could
hold in his mouth and jump off the cart and run home
with them. He took a little mouthful of fish and the

driver did not look round. He took a bigger mouthful of fish and the driver did not look round. Danny Fox watched him for a moment and saw that his hair was black and curly. He looked young and slim and strong.

'What a pity,' thought Danny. 'I wish he was old and slow!' And he lay down very quietly, hoping not to wake him. And crunch, crunch, crunch, he took a great big noisy mouthful and the driver jumped up and brought his whip down – swish! – on the white tip of his tail. Danny Fox leapt off the cart and over a stone wall into a field.

Now he was very unhappy. He had eaten three mouthfuls of fish, but had nothing to bring home to Lick, Chew, and Swallow, and nothing for Doxie either. The cart had gone on but – 'sniff, sniff, sniff' – he could still smell the fish as he lay hiding behind the wall.

He lay and he lay and he thought and he thought, till he thought of a plan. Then he got up quickly and he ran and he ran, keeping close behind the wall so that the driver of the cart could not see him. He ran till he came to a place where the road turned a corner, and by now the cart was far behind him. Then he jumped over the wall and lay down in the middle of the road pretending to be dead.

He lay there a long time. He heard the cart coming nearer and nearer. He kept his eyes shut. He hoped the driver would see him and not run him over.

When the driver saw Danny lying stretched in the middle of the road, he stopped his cart and said, 'That's funny. That's the fox that was stealing my fish. That's the fox I hit with my whip. I thought I had only touched the tip of his tail, but now I see I must have hurt him badly. He must have run away from me ahead of my cart. And now he is dead.' He got down from his cart and stooped to look at Danny.

'What a beautiful red coat he's got,' the driver said, 'and what beautiful, thick red trousers. What a beautiful long bushy tail, with a beautiful white tip. What a beautiful long smooth nose with a beautiful black tip. I'll take him home with me, I think, and skin him and sell his fur.'

So he picked up Danny Fox and threw him on to the cart on top of the boxes of fish. The cart went on. Danny opened one eye and saw the driver's back was turned to

him. Then very quietly, he slid the tip of his tail underneath a fish and flicked it on to the road. He lay quite still and threw another fish out with his tail, then another and another and another, till all down the road behind the cart there was a long, long line of fish stretching into the distance. And the driver never looked round because he thought Danny was dead. At the next corner, Danny jumped off the cart and ran back down the road. When the cart was out of sight, he started to pick the fish up.

16

He picked up one for Lick. He picked up one for
Chew. He picked up one for Swallow. He tried to pick
up one for Doxie too but his mouth was too full, so off
he ran towards home with three fishes' heads sticking out
from one side of his mouth and three fishes' tails sticking
out from the other.

He ran past the farm, and the duck and the goose and the hen were watching him.

'Look out,' said the duck. 'There goes Danny Fox!'

'That's funny,' said the goose, 'he has grown new whiskers.'

'Those aren't whiskers,' said the hen.

'Yes, they are,' said the goose.

'No, they're not,' said the hen.

'What are they, then?' said the duck.

'They are three fishes' heads on one side of his mouth,' said the hen, 'and three fishes' tails on the other.'

Danny ran along the bottom of the mountain past the mouse's hole. The mouse was peeping out.

'That's funny,' said the mouse. 'I can see three fishes running along. But they have legs like a fox.'

'Fishes don't have legs,' said the pigeon who was flying up above.

'Yes, they do,' said the mouse.

'No, they don't,' said the pigeon.

'These ones do,' said the mouse.

Danny Fox ran up the mountain past the crack in the rocks where the rabbit was hiding.

'That's funny,' said the rabbit. 'Danny Fox has been out fishing. I didn't know he had a boat.'

At last Danny reached home. He threw one fish to Lick, and one fish to Chew and one fish to Swallow and while they were licking and chewing and swallowing he said to their mother, 'Come quickly with me.'

Doxie and Danny Fox ran down the mountain again till they came to the road – and after they had eaten three fish each, they picked up three fish each and carried them home. Then they went back for another three fish each, and another three fish each and another three fish each. They went on all morning carrying fish up the mountain, until there were no more left on the road.

So Danny and Doxie and Lick and Chew and Swallow had an enormous feast. They ate and they ate until they could eat no more. Then they all fell down together in a heap, fast asleep.

2. Danny Tricks the Fisherman

While Danny and Doxie were picking the fish up from the road, the cart went on towards the town. The driver with the curly black hair was a young fisherman who had been out all night fishing on the sea. When he reached the market square in the middle of the town, he looked up at one of the windows of the tallest building and made a secret sign. The tallest building was the Royal Palace, and from the window, every morning, the Princess waved to him.

Then the fisherman began to shout, 'Come buy my fresh fish. Fresh mackerel and herring! Come buy my fresh fish, caught early this morning!' and the people came running out of their houses with dishes and pans for the fish and money for him. But when they saw there were no fish on the cart they began to laugh, and other people came running into the street to see what they were laughing at until the poor fisherman and his horse and cart were surrounded by a crowd of laughing people. He stood up on the cart and said, 'It isn't right to laugh at me.' But the people said, 'You have no fish. Why did you call to us to buy your fresh fish when you haven't any?'

'I caught a lot of fish last night,' said the man. 'My cart was filled with fish.'

But the people said, 'We don't believe you.'

Then he told them how he had found a large dead fox and thrown him on to the cart.

'Then where is the dead fox?' the people said. 'Your cart is empty.'

'He must have come alive again and eaten all my fish.'

This made the people laugh again. Only the Princess waved from her window in the palace to show she believed what he said.

The poor young fisherman had to drive all the way home without earning any money. He said to himself, 'If I see that fox again, I'll catch him. Then I'll take him to the town and show him to the people and make them believe I am telling the truth.'

He went home and lit the fire and sat beside it thinking of ways to catch Danny Fox.

His house was small. It had a front door opening out on to the beach and a back door leading to a stony footpath which went up the mountain towards Danny Fox's den. But whichever door you went in by, you found yourself in the same room; because there was only one room in the house. The back door had a hole at the bottom to allow the fisherman's dog to come in and out. The fisherman's bed was beside the back door against the wall.

He felt tired because he had been out fishing all night, so after he had warmed himself at the fire, he took off his clothes and went to bed. He lay in bed thinking, 'I wish Danny Fox would walk into my house. Then I'd catch him. If only wishes came true!' And then he felt very tired and fell asleep. He slept until the evening.

Danny Fox had eaten so many fish in the morning that he fell asleep till the evening too. Then, just as the sun was going down, he went for a walk. He walked and walked till he came to the farm. And the duck and the goose and the hen were watching him.

'Look out,' said the duck, 'there goes Danny Fox.'

'That's funny,' said the goose, 'he has swallowed a football.'

'That's not a football,' said the hen.

'Yes, it is,' said the goose.

'No, it's not,' said the hen.

'What is it, then?' said the duck.

'It is all the fish he has eaten,' said the hen, 'making his tummy bulge.'

Danny walked past the mouse's hole. The mouse was peeping out.

'That's funny,' said the mouse, 'I can see a football rolling along. But it's got legs like a fox.'

But an old mother ewe, who was there on the mountain path, said, 'That's not a football; that's a fox, and I'm not going to let him come any farther in case he tries to take my lamb away.'

When Danny Fox heard this he walked up to the old mother ewe and said, 'You needn't worry, Mother Ewe. I won't take your lamb. I am not a bit hungry. And

24

Doxie's not hungry, because we've got plenty of fish. So please let me pass.'

But the old mother ewe would not believe him. She stood in the middle of the path and lowered her head. She was ready to butt him. Danny Fox could easily have got past her by stepping off the path into the heather. But he felt cross because she would not step to one side and let him pass.

'Get out of my way,' he said. 'Or I'll bite you.'

'Go back the way you came,' she said, 'or I'll butt you and trample on you with my hoofs.'

Danny Fox growled fiercely. The old mother ewe made a rush at him, but he jumped on to her back and tried to bite her. His teeth sank into her thick wool and did not hurt her a bit, but he would not let go.

'If he holds on like this,' thought the old mother ewe, 'I can carry him away from this place.' She started to

run down the mountain path towards the beach, with the fox clinging on to her wool. She ran very fast.

Danny Fox didn't mind. He enjoyed the ride. He said to himself, 'She will soon get tired and then she will have to go back up the mountain to the place where she lives and I won't let go till she brings me back.'

But the path led down to the fisherman's house near the beach, and when they got there the old ewe started baaing for help. The fisherman was still asleep and did not hear her.

'Get off my back,' she said. Danny knew that if he spoke he would have to let go, so he did not answer.

'If I carry you home and stop outside your den, will you let go?'

He gave a tug at her wool, which meant 'Yes'.

'Then I'll start running,' she said, 'and I won't stop till I'm outside your den.'

But instead of running up the mountain again she ran round and round the fisherman's house. Round and round and round she ran until Danny Fox began to feel giddy. Round and round and round she ran until the sun had gone right down and everything was dark. Round and round and round she ran, till Danny Fox was so giddy he thought he would have to let go. Then suddenly she stopped outside the fisherman's back door. Danny Fox was glad to let go. He slid off her back on to the ground. Now he was so giddy that he couldn't stand straight. He wobbled and staggered and, instead of going round and

round the fisherman's house, the fisherman's house went round and round him.

'Where am I?' he thought. 'The old ewe stopped and now she has run off. Am I really outside my den?' Then he saw the hole at the bottom of the fisherman's back door. Light from the fire shone through it. 'Can that be the entrance to my den? Where is Doxie? Where is Lick? Where is Chew? Where is Swallow? Oh I do wish the entrance to our den would stay still. Next time it comes round I'll go in.'

When he went into the fisherman's house, he knew how the old ewe had tricked him, but he was still feeling giddy and the fire was warm, so he sat down beside it to wait till his giddiness stopped. He did not see the fisherman, who was lying on the bed. But when he picked up some sticks with his mouth and threw them on to the fire to make it blaze, the fisherman woke up.

'Ha, ha,' said the fisherman, 'now I have caught you. My wish has come true.'

'You haven't caught me yet,' said Danny Fox, and he jumped up and made a dash for the hole in the door.

But because he was still a bit giddy, he went to the wrong door first – to the front door, which had no hole in it. And the fisherman jumped out of bed and sat down on the floor by the back door, blocking the hole.

'Now,' said the fisherman, 'you're a prisoner. You can't get out of here. And when my dog comes home we'll catch you together.'

'No you won't,' said Danny Fox, 'because I've got a plan to make you get up from that hole in the door.'

Danny Fox walked round the room sniffing. He walked on the tips of his toes and his claws went click click on the stone floor. He found the fisherman's shoes. 'If I put these on the fire,' thought Danny Fox, 'he's sure to get up to save them from being burned.' So he walked to the fire-place with the shoes in his mouth and threw them into the blaze.

'I will not get up,' said the fisherman. 'I will go fishing in my bare feet.'

Danny Fox found his coat and threw it on the fire.

'I will not get up,' said the fisherman. 'I will go fishing without my coat.'

Danny Fox found his shirt and threw it on the fire.

'I will not get up,' said the fisherman. 'I will go fishing without my shirt.'

Danny Fox found his vest and threw it on the fire.

'I will not get up,' said the fisherman. 'I will go fishing without my vest.'

Danny Fox found his pants and threw them on the fire.

'I will not get up,' said the fisherman. 'I will go fishing without my pants.'

Danny Fox found his trousers and threw them on the fire, but still the fisherman sat blocking the hole in the door.

'My trousers are old and torn, anyway,' he said. 'I will not get up for them. I will wrap a blanket round me and go fishing.'

Then Danny Fox saw a fishing net lying in the corner of the room. He started to drag it towards the fire. The fisherman shouted, 'No! No! No! I can't go fishing without that.' And he ran across the room and grabbed the net. Danny Fox let go at once and ran like a red streak out through the hole in the door.

When the fisherman's dog came home and saw what

had happened to his master's clothes, he was very angry. He went to the farmer and told him what had happened, and the farmer said, 'I've got plenty of coats and trousers and vests and pants and shoes. Here you are. Take these home to your master.'

The fisherman was happy when he saw the new clothes. But he said, 'One day, I shall catch Danny Fox.'

3. Danny Meets the Princess

It was in the middle of the night when Danny got home. Lick, Chew, and Swallow had been sound asleep all the time, but poor Mrs Doxie Fox lay awake worrying because Danny was away so long.

'What have you been doing?' she said when she saw him.

'Nothing much,' said Danny and he gave a big yawn to show he didn't want to talk. He was afraid she might laugh at him if she heard how the old mother ewe had tricked him. He made a yowling kind of noise when he yawned and his white teeth shone in the darkness.

'Well, you haven't been out hunting, I should think,' said Mrs Doxie Fox. 'Not after all that fish.'

'No, I haven't been out hunting,' said Danny Fox and this time he shook himself and sneezed to show he didn't want to talk, and when he shook himself a cloud of ashes from the fisherman's fireplace flew out of his coat and made Mrs Doxie Fox sneeze too. He sneezed and she sneezed and she sneezed and he sneezed and they both sneezed together and made such a noise that the children woke up, and Lick and Chew sneezed and Swallow sneezed too. And then Mr Danny Fox and Mrs Doxie Fox and Lick, Chew, and Swallow all sneezed together, and made such a loud noise that all the animals and birds who stay awake at night – such as the mouse and the rat and the owl and the cat, and the nightjar and the bat, and the polecat, the nightingale and mole, and water-vole, and the weasel and the hedgehog, and the badger and the bull-frog – left whatever they were doing and came to the door of the foxes' den to listen. And this is what they heard:

'I can smell burning!' (It was Lick who said that.)

'It's someone's fur burning!' (It was Chew who said that.)

'It's Daddy. It's Daddy. Oh Mummy, he's on fire!' It was Swallow who said that in his high yelping voice.

'He's not on fire,' said Mrs Doxie Fox. 'But, Danny I'm afraid you've singed your beautiful red coat, and, oh, you are covered with ashy dust. A-tishoo!'

'If I've singed my red coat, said Danny Fox, 'it is because I'm the bravest and cleverest creature in the world.'

'Oh yes! You are brave and clever,' said the children. 'Oh tell us what you have done.'

So he told them how he had escaped from the fisherman's house.

'I think you are too brave and clever,' said Mrs Doxie Fox. 'If you think you are so brave and clever, one day you'll be caught.'

When the animals and birds who were crouching at the door heard her say that, they laughed loudly. And when Danny Fox heard them he rushed out barking and snarling and curling up his lip to show his fierce white teeth. Those who could run ran away and those who could

hop hopped away, and those who could fly flew away. No one was brave enough to laugh while Danny Fox was near. And Danny walked back into his den, very stiffly and proudly with the hair of his neck and back standing up on end. He circled round and round, scratching the floor with his paw, then curled himself up to sleep, with his nose tucked under his hind leg and his long bushy tail round his face like a scarf. Mrs Doxie Fox cuddled her children till they were asleep again. Then at last she went to sleep too.

Danny Fox was the first to wake up in the morning. Just as the sun began to rise he walked down the mountain path, sniffing the morning air and standing still every now and then on three legs, with one front paw dangling, to look into the distance. He saw the fisherman's cottage below him and beyond it the sea, which was pale bluey grey, with a long bright streak across it, like a golden river. The golden river was really the sunlight reflected on the water as on a mirror. The sun had just come up on the horizon. Only half of it showed above the water, like half a plate made of gold. In the middle of the sea, a long, long way away Danny Fox saw a dark blue blob sticking up out of the water. He did not know what it was. Whenever he went for a walk he looked at everything, the near things and the far things, and if he didn't know what something was, he felt secretly frightened. But he never told anyone that. If the thing moved he was very frightened. If it didn't move he was only a little bit frightened. The dark blue thing sticking out of the sea did not move at all because it was an island. But Danny Fox was a little bit frightened because he didn't know what an island was.

Then he heard a noise quite near him, and smelled a smell he had never smelt before, and saw a strange thing bobbing up and down behind a rock. The noise was made by the Princess. She had knelt down behind the rock to watch him and by mistake her knee had touched a dry twig which broke with a crack. The smell was the smell of a precious scent called *Crêpe de Chine* which she dabbed behind her ears every morning. And the strange thing which Danny Fox saw bobbing up and down behind the rock was the crown she wore on her head. The Princess had never been so near a wild fox before and she was trying to hide from him and to watch him at the same time. She thought him beautiful.

Danny backed away a little bit to be ready to run if the strange object was very dangerous, or charge forward and bite it if it was only a little bit dangerous. But when the Princess walked out from behind the rock, he wasn't a bit afraid. She had a bunch of wild flowers in one hand and a basket full of mushrooms in the other.

'Good morning, Mr Fox,' she said.

'Good morning, your majesty the Queen,' said Danny, looking at her crown.

'I'm not the Queen,' the Princess said.

'But you're wearing a crown!' said Danny Fox.

'I am the Princess. Princesses wear crowns, you know.'

'I think foxes should wear crowns,' said Danny Fox.

The Princess laughed. 'Why should foxes wear crowns?' she said.

'I'll ask you a riddle and then you'll see why,' said Danny Fox. 'Why is a fox like a princess?'

The Princess could not answer.

'Because he can do just as he likes,' said Danny Fox. 'There is nobody to order him about.'

'Princesses can't do as they like,' the Princess said. 'Look at me – I have to obey the Queen.'

'Are you afraid of her?'

'Yes,' said the Princess. 'She is my stepmother. She's very strict with me.'

'I'm not afraid of anyone,' said Danny Fox. 'May I try on your crown?'

'Yes,' said the Princess, taking it off her head. 'Let me see if it will fit you. But you won't bite, will you?'

'Of course not,' said Danny.

'I'm sorry I mentioned it,' the Princess said, 'but I've always heard that foxes are full of tricks.'

'Oh yes, that's true,' said Danny Fox proudly. 'I am always full of tricks. I'm the cleverest creature at tricks in all the world.'

The Princess stepped back from him and said, 'Oh then, if you try my crown on, you'll run away with it!'

'No, I won't. I never play tricks on people I like.'

'Do you like me?' said the Princess.

'Yes,' said Danny Fox.

'Oh good!' she said. 'Then I'll put the crown on your head. Will you promise not to bite?'

'I promise not to bite.'

Danny Fox's head was too small, so she put it round his neck and he wore it as a necklace for a few minutes, walking round and round her proudly. Then he stopped and asked her, 'How do I look?'

She laughed and said, 'Well, you don't look at all like a Princess or a Queen.'

'Tell me why you are afraid of the Queen,' said Danny Fox.

'Well, I'll tell you a secret if you like . . .' the Princess said.

'Yes, please,' said Danny Fox.

'But first of all, please give me back my crown.' She took the crown from him and put it back on her head. Then she said, 'My stepmother, the Queen, won't let me marry the man I love.'

'And who is he?' said Danny Fox.

'Can you keep a secret?' the Princess said.

Instead of answering, Danny wagged his tail.

'I want to marry a fisherman,' the Princess said.

Danny Fox's tail stopped wagging. He looked at her suspiciously, but she wasn't looking at him any more.

'I must go home to breakfast now,' she said.

When he heard the word breakfast, Danny Fox began to feel hungry. 'What are you having for breakfast?' he said.

'These mushrooms,' she said. 'Would you like some? I gathered them this morning. They are beautifully fresh. They're still covered with dew.'

'No, thank you,' said Danny because he felt proud. 'No, thank you, I'm having an egg.

'An egg!' said the Princess.

'Yes, an egg.'

'But how can you, up here on the mountain? How can you find an egg?'

'It is easy,' said Danny Fox, holding his head very high.

'I'm afraid you will steal it,' the Princess said.

'No, no, a friend of mine will give it to me as a present. Are you a friend of mine?' said Danny Fox, and he held his head on one side and looked at her, standing on three legs again and letting one paw dangle in the air.

'I don't know,' said the Princess gaily. 'But anyway I haven't got an egg.' Then she laughed and ran away.

4. Danny Flies Away

The whole of the sun had risen above the sea by now, but it was not yet high in the sky, and the shadows it cast on the mountainside were very long. Even a small stone had a shadow ten times as big as itself and Danny Fox, when he looked at his own shadow, was prouder of himself than ever, because his legs seemed longer than a wolf's, the shadows of his teeth were like long daggers, and his ears looked big and frightening like sharp horns. But suddenly the whole lovely, big, fierce shadow of Danny Fox was blotted out by a really terrible shadow that came down from something in the sky. Danny Fox crouched with his tummy to the ground and crept into a big clump of whins. He sniffed and he sniffed and he lay down on the prickly ground beneath the whinbush and rested his chin on the back of his front paws, and he sniffed. He peered and peered out from a gap between the yellow flowers of the whin and he saw the shadow of a bird with two gigantic wings.

'Sniff, sniff,' said Danny in the whinbush, and the prickles were prickling his tummy. 'Sniff, sniff. I can sniff an eagle, and even if the shadow of that eagle is ten times as big as the eagle, I'm going to hide here till he's gone.'

The King Eagle, the golden eagle, whose wings if he stretched them out from tip to tip would reach from the pillow to the foot of a grown-up person's bed, had seen Danny Fox and decided to give him a fright. He knew, and Danny knew, that the golden eagle is the only bird strong enough and brave enough to pounce down from the sky on a fox and pick him up in his claws and fly away with him. But the King Eagle didn't want to do that. He only hovered over Danny Fox for fun . . . to see what Danny would do when he was frightened. And Danny hid under the whinbush until he was sure that the eagle had flown far away.

But the King Eagle, without knowing it, had given Danny a bright idea.

Danny Fox's black shiny wet nose came out between the thorns and the bright yellow flowers of the whinbush and as soon as he had made sure he could not smell the eagle any more, he put his eyes out too, then his ears and the whole of his head and he saw the King Eagle flying high in the sky towards the sea coast, going farther and farther and farther along by the side of the beach till he was like a small black bird, the size of a blackbird, a sparrow, a robin, and at last a tiny wren.

Danny Fox now felt very safe and brave and galloped along and galloped along, up and up the mountain path, galloping, galloping, up, up, and up, through stones and rocks and gravel and heather and damp mossy places and dry lichen places till he came to the crag at the top of the mountain where he knew that the eagle had built his nest. Then he sat on a tuffet of grass, curled the white tip of his tail round his ankles, and licked his lips.

'I wish the Princess could see me now!' he said to

himself. 'I wish the Princess could watch my friend giving me an egg for my breakfast.'

Then he looked up towards the top of the crag – a high precipice impossible to climb – and pointing his nose up in the air he uttered a strange, frightening cry – 'Oo–loo–loo–oo!' All the birds of the air and the animals of the mountain stood still when they heard Danny Fox. Then they all ran away and hid. But the Queen Eagle, who was safely on her nest on top of the great rocky crag which no one could climb, just sat on her eggs feeling happy and safe.

Danny Fox knew exactly where her nest was. He knew he could never climb up to it. He knew the Queen Eagle was strong enough to fight him. But he thought, 'Perhaps she is stupid.' He thought, 'I am the cleverest creature in the world. Let me see how stupid the Queen Eagle is.'

Then he called out to her, 'My friend!' She looked

down from her nest and saw him far below, but she did not answer because she knew he was not her friend.

Then Danny Fox shouted, 'Your Majesty!'

'Yes?' said the Queen Eagle.

'Throw me down one of your eggs for breakfast.'

'No,' said the Queen Eagle.

'You'd better,' said Danny Fox.

'Certainly not,' said the Queen Eagle.

Danny Fox put on his deepest, gruffest voice and shouted, 'Then look out! I'm going to knock down the whole crag, and get all your eggs.'

'Oh please don't do that!' the Queen Eagle screamed.

'Yes, I will.'

'But my lovely nest will be broken! My precious eggs all smashed!'

'Then throw me one down.'

The stupid Queen Eagle believed that Danny would be able to knock the crag down. She thought it would be better to give away one egg than to see them all

smashed on the ground, so she sadly threw one down. Danny caught it in his mouth and ate it for his breakfast.

The eagle's egg was delicious and next morning when the King Eagle was away hunting, Danny Fox came and threatened her again. She threw him down another egg. And the next morning he came and threatened her again and she threw him down another egg. So now the poor Queen Eagle had only three eggs left instead of six.

When the King Eagle's turn came to sit on the eggs and keep them warm he said, 'What's this? We used to have six eggs and now there are only three.' And when the Queen Eagle told him what had happened he was very angry. First he was cross with her for having been so stupid. 'You ought to have known that a fox couldn't knock down a huge crag of rock like this,' he said. 'You ought to have known that a fox is full of tricks.' Then he was very angry with Danny Fox. And on the fourth morning, instead of going hunting, he hid by the nest and waited to see what would happen. Danny Fox could only see the Queen Eagle.

'Hullo, your Majesty, I'm here,' he shouted.

'Say "Go away,"' the King Eagle whispered to his wife.

'Go away, Danny Fox,' she screamed from the top of the crag.

'I'll knock the crag down,' shouted Danny.

'Say "You're not strong enough,"' the King Eagle whispered.

'You can't – you're not strong enough,' she screamed.

'Throw down an egg or I'll knock the crag down.'

'Say "Knock it down then,"' the King Eagle whispered.

'Knock it down then!' she screamed from the top of the crag.

Then Danny Fox saw the King Eagle fly out from his hiding place beside the nest. He was very annoyed. He knew the King Eagle was not stupid. He knew he would get no more eggs. 'But I'm cleverer than him,' he said to himself. 'I'll lie down here and pretend to be dead, and when he comes near to look at me I'll snap him by the neck and kill him. Then his stupid wife will give me the rest of her eggs.'

So Danny Fox lay down at the foot of the crag and pretended to be dead. He lay so still for such a long time that the King Eagle thought, 'Perhaps he really is dead. Perhaps he was frightened to death when he saw me.'

The Eagle flew nearer and nearer to Danny Fox to see whether he was dead. Danny Fox lay absolutely still. 'I don't think he's really dead,' the Eagle said to himself. 'I'll test him.' And then he spoke aloud so that Danny Fox could hear.

'Dead foxes always move one ear,' he said.

When Danny heard this he moved one ear.

'Dead foxes always wag their tails,' the Eagle said.

When Danny heard this he wagged his bushy tail.

'Dead foxes always twitch their hind legs,' the Eagle said.

When Danny heard this he twitched his hind legs.

'Dead foxes always raise their front paws in the air,' the Eagle said.

When Danny heard this he raised his front paws in the air.

'Dead foxes always shut one eye,' the Eagle said.

When Danny heard this he shut one eye.

'Dead foxes always shut both eyes,' the Eagle said.

When Danny heard this, he shut both eyes.

'DEAD FOXES ALWAYS KEEP THEIR MOUTHS TIGHT SHUT!' the Eagle said, and when he heard this Danny Fox shut his mouth and kept it tight shut and the Eagle swooped down and picked him up in his great claws and flew away with him. He carried him high in the sky and flew faster and faster and farther and farther away from the nest. At first, when Danny Fox got over his surprise, he quite enjoyed the ride. 'They say animals can't fly,' he said to himself. 'But it's really not so very difficult for a clever fox like me.' But when he looked down and saw that they were over the sea, he began to be afraid the Eagle might drop him. He was afraid he would drown.

Then in the distance he saw the blue blob he had seen one morning sticking out of the sea. They came nearer and nearer to it, until it didn't look blue at all. It looked grey. It looked like a huge flat piece of rock. They got nearer and nearer and nearer to the rocky island and at last, just as they were flying over it, the Eagle let go of Danny Fox. Danny Fox fell whizzing through the air and landed on his feet on the island, very surprised.

'You just stay there, Mr Danny Fox,' the Eagle called to him. 'And not be any more nuisance.'

'Oh *please*,' called Danny. 'Don't leave me here! How can I get home across all that sea?'

But the King Eagle seemed not to hear him. He was flying away high in the sky towards his nest on the mountain, farther and farther across the sea till he looked like a small black bird, the size of a blackbird, a sparrow, a tiny wren, until at last Danny Fox could see him no more.

5. Danny Is Marooned

Danny Fox was hungry. He hadn't had his usual Eagle's egg. In fact, he hadn't had any breakfast at all, and on the little island he couldn't see anything except grey rock and he couldn't smell anything that smelt like food. When he put his nose in the air to sniff for food the wind was so strong that he could hardly breathe. He turned his back to the wind and sniffed towards the middle of the island.

'Sniff, sniff,' he said, 'I can only sniff fresh air.'

Then he turned his left side to the wind and the wind ruffled his red coat, showing a yellow furry lining underneath, and he sniffed towards the beach.

'Sniff, sniff,' he said, 'I can only sniff seaweed.'

Then he turned his right side to the wind and the wind ruffled the other side of his red coat, showing another bit of yellow furry lining, and he sniffed towards the other part of the beach.

'Sniff, sniff,' he said, 'I can only sniff seaweed there too.'

'Don't you like the smell of seaweed?' said a voice.

'Only after breakfast,' Danny Fox said. He put his head on one side to listen. Then he looked all about him and turned round and round, but he couldn't see anyone at all. He couldn't smell anyone either.

'Who's there?' he said. 'Sniff, sniff. I can only sniff fresh air.'

'Don't you like fresh air?' said the voice.

'After meals it's all right,' said Danny Fox. 'But if you have too much of it, it makes you hungry.'

'Why don't you shut your nostrils then, until you've caught a fish?'

'Shut my nostrils?' said Danny. 'I can keep my mouth shut sometimes, but not my nostrils.'

'You can't be much of an animal,' said the voice.

'And you're not much,' said Danny Fox, 'because I can't even see you. And I can't smell you. You are nothing.'

'Can't you open your eyes?'

'Of course I can open my eyes.'

'And shut them?'

'Of course I can.'

'But not your nostrils? You can't open and shut your nostrils!' said the voice and laughed at him.

'Of course not,' said Danny Fox crossly. 'Nobody can.'

'Sea animals can,' said the voice. 'Just open your eyes and look down at the water.'

Danny Fox heard a noise of someone blowing bubbles under water. Then he trotted down over the rocks to the edge of the sea, with his long smooth nose stretched out in front of him and his bushy tail stretched out behind, and he saw a round head which seemed to be floating on the sea, with two brown eyes that gazed at him and a wide whiskery mouth.

'Sniff, sniff,' said Danny Fox. 'I can smell fish.'

'No, you can't,' said the whiskery mouth in the sea, 'you can probably sniff me, because I eat so many fish. I am a seal, a *Phoca barbata*.'

'I beg your pardon,' said Danny. He was always very keen to learn words he'd never heard before. He liked to go home and use the new words when he spoke to Lick, Chew, and Swallow. He liked to hear them say, 'What does that mean?' and then he would tell them the meaning.

'What does that mean?' he said to the whiskery head.

'A *Phoca barbata* is a seal – a bearded seal, one of the largest of all the seals – and one of the fattest. You'd better remember that, because if you're going to live on this island you may need me.'

'Did I hear you mention catching fish?' said Danny Fox. He put on the sweetest voice he could imagine. He was trying to talk like the Princess. But the seal said, 'Why are you talking in that funny way? Watch my nose.'

'Oh yes,' said Danny Fox. 'I'd love to watch your nose.' He watched it and saw how the seal could take a deep, long breath with his nostrils wide open, and then close them tight, as anyone else might close his mouth.

'I do that when I dive down into the sea,' said the seal. 'I can hold my breath under the water for twenty minutes.'

'How many fish can you catch in twenty minutes?' said Danny Fox.

'Only one at a time, you silly,' said the seal making a very loud noise.

'I meant,' said Danny, 'that if you could catch more than you want yourself, it might be a good plan to throw the rest up here on to the island.'

'For you to eat?' said the seal.

'Maybe I'll eat them,' said Danny Fox. 'I don't like anything to go to waste.'

'Just like a land animal,' said the seal.

'What's like a land animal?'

'Fussing over things like waste,' said the seal.

'I'm not fussing – I'm hungry.'

'Well, you can have what I usually throw away. Do you care for salmon?'

'Yes, please,' said Danny Fox.

'I only like one bite from each. I'll give you the rest. I'll go and catch one,' said the seal, and as his whiskery grey head sank under the water, the flippers of his hind legs flapped on the top and splashed Danny Fox with salt water.

While he was away Danny Fox looked sadly out across the sea. First he thought, 'How shall I ever get home?'

Then as he grew hungrier he thought, 'I shall never see Doxie or Lick, Chew, and Swallow again.' Then as he grew hungrier and hungrier and hungrier he thought, 'That seal is not coming back. I can feel myself shrinking. I'm thinner and thinner. I shall die of starvation and no one will know.'

He heard a loud splashing and grunting and there was the seal with a salmon in its mouth.

'There you are,' he said, 'I've had all I want.'

'Oh thank you, Mr Phoca Barbata,' said Danny and began to eat.

'You remembered my name very well.'

'I've got a good memory,' said Danny, with his mouth full. 'In fact, I've got a better memory than anyone else in the world.'

The seal snorted rudely.

'I wanted to tell your name to my children,' said Danny Fox. 'But the sad thing is I shall never see them again.' He took another big mouthful of fish.

'Why won't you see them again?' said the seal.

'Because they're on the other side of all that sea.'

'Can't you swim?' said the seal.

'Not all that way,' said Danny Fox.

The seal began to laugh at him again. 'You land animals can't do much,' he said.

'Of course I *could* swim home, if I wanted to,' said Danny when he'd finished choking on a bone. 'But Mrs Doxie Fox would be very upset if I spoiled my red coat with salt water.'

'Of course,' said the seal, pretending to believe him, because really he hated to hurt anybody's feelings – though often he couldn't stop himself in time.

'But you mentioned land animals just now,' said Danny Fox, and he swallowed down his last mouthful. 'And it seems to me you don't know much about them. Because land animals are cleverer than sea animals, and

quicker and funnier and happier, and their dreams are far more beautiful and more exciting.'

'How do you know?' said the seal.

'Because I am the cleverest and quickest and funniest and happiest of them all – and anyway there are more of them.'

'More what?' said the seal.

'More land animals than sea animals,' said Danny Fox. He picked up a pebble in his mouth and tossed it in the air.

'You are wrong,' said the seal.

'There are more different kinds of animals on the land than in the sea,' said Danny Fox.

'There are more different kinds of animals in the sea than on the land,' said the seal.

'No, there aren't,' said Danny Fox.

'Yes, there are,' said the seal.

'No, there aren't.'

'Yes, there are.'

'No, there aren't.'

'Yes, there are,' said the seal.

'Then bring them here, for me to count them,' said Danny Fox. 'How far would your sea animals stretch if you told them to line up?'

'A long way.'

'As far as that land over there, where my home is?'

'Much farther than that,' said the seal.

'Then go and fetch them all,' said Danny Fox. 'I want to count them.'

'But how shall I count the land animals?' said the seal.

'Don't worry, Mr Phoca Barbata,' said Danny Fox. 'As soon as I've counted your lot, I'll fetch mine.'

'All right,' said the seal. 'I'll fetch them, but I'll have to go all round the world. I'll be away a long time.'

'Then leave a store of fish for me,' said Danny, shouting after him. But the seal had dived underwater and did not hear. He began to swim around the world. 'Follow me,' he said to all the sea animals, and every day new kinds swam after him until he was the leader of a long procession.

Day after day went by and Danny had nothing to eat.

He got thinner and thinner and colder and colder. There was no den to keep the wind away. No tree for shelter. Not even a bush to hide in. And Danny Fox grew weak and miserable. The hairs fell out of his bushy tail. His

fine red coat grew dull and sparse and his ribs and hip bones began to show through it. His shiny black nose became dry and rough and his bright, sharp eyes were dim. But half the time he kept saying to himself, 'I'm the cleverest and quickest and happiest of all the animals on earth and my dreams are so exciting that I can forget about food.' And half the time he kept saying to himself,

'But all the same food is better than dreams – or at least it's best to have both. And I wish I'd told that seal to go only half way round the world. Will he ever come back? Will he ever come back?'

Then one day, after a long, long time, just as he was saying that, he heard the bubbling noise again, and the seal had come back. And the seal said, 'Half way round the world! You stupid fox. If I went half way round the world and turned back, I'd still have to come the same distance to get home. I thought you said you were clever. Oh you do look thin! Here's a fish for you.'

For once, Danny Fox didn't answer back. He gobbled up the fish.

6. Danny's Bridge Across the Sea

'Now,' said the seal. 'You think there are more kinds of animals on the land than in the sea. Don't you?'

'Yes,' said Danny Fox with his mouth full.

'Well,' said the seal. 'When you've finished eating, look over there.'

Danny Fox finished eating and looked up and saw a mighty commotion in the sea. One minute it was full of bobbing heads and splashing bodies like a crowded swimming pool, and the next minute it was bubbling and squirting and gushing and swashing like a washing machine full of different coloured clothes. The highest squirts came from the whales who blew tall fountains of water into the air and the longest line of splashes came from the dolphins who jumped in and out of the water as they raced along. And all the other animals that lived in the sea were playing and gurgling or fighting and squalling or bubbling and slushing and squishing and squashing, or fishing and guzzling or pushing and nuzzling or cuddling or muddling and paddling and puddling along.

Danny Fox couldn't tell whether he was watching a million animals all jumbled up, or one immense animal that kept on falling to bits and joining together again.

'Well, count them,' said the seal.

'How can I count that muddle?' said Danny Fox. 'Line them up and tell them to keep still.'

The seal began to line them up round the shore of the island with their noses to the beach. But he told the whales not to come too near.

'If they run aground in shallow water we shall never get them off again,' he said to Danny Fox.

'I quite agree, Mr Phoca Barbata,' said Danny. 'In fact I think it is dangerous for any of these animals to come near the shore.'

'The seals don't mind,' said the seal. 'We can walk on the land quite well.'

'How many kinds of seals have you brought?' said Danny Fox.

'I've brought the common seal, and the fur seal and the hair seal and the harp seal and the golden seal.'

'Tell the common seal to put his front feet on the beach,' said Danny Fox. 'The fur seal and the hair seal and the harp seal and the golden seal can line up behind him in the sea. Then some other animals can go behind them until the line reaches water deep enough for whales.'

'And I've brought the marbled seal, the monk seal, the Atlantic grey seal and the elephant seal and the bottle-nosed seal,' said the seal.

'The bottle-nosed seal?' said Danny Fox, with his head on one side.

'And the sea leopard – and that's all the seals I've brought.'

'The sea leopard? What's that?' said Danny Fox.

'It's another name for the South Sea seal,' said the seal. 'You've heard of the sea lion, I suppose?'

'Of course,' said Danny Fox.

'Nearly all sea animals have two names,' said the seal. 'And one of those names comes from a land animal.'

'Tell the sea leopard to swim to that land over there where my home is and put his front paws on the beach,' said Danny Fox, 'and the marble and monk and elephant and grey and bottle-nose can line up behind him. Then if all the others can bridge the gap between those two lots of seals I'll admit there are more animals in the sea than on the land.'

'You've got to count them,' said the seal. 'Like you said.'

'Of course I'll count them,' said Danny Fox.

'But how will you see to count them over all that sea?' said the seal.

'Just do what I tell you, Mr Phoca Barbata,' said Danny Fox. 'And you'll find out how I count them.'

Then the seal began calling for the sea mouse and the sea lion, the sea elephant, the sea cow, the sea dog, the sea otter, the sea wolf, the sea unicorn and . . .

'That's not fair,' said Danny Fox. 'You can't have magic or fairy-tale animals.'

'It's not magic,' said the seal. 'The sea unicorn is the Narwhal – that lumpy creature over there, with a long horn like a corkscrew on his snout.'

Danny looked at this creature and saw that it was large enough for him to stand on.

'All right,' he said, 'tell the Narwhal to line up.'

Then the seal called for the sea parrot and the sea swallow, the sea robin, the sea raven, and the sea canary.

'Those are birds. It's not fair,' said Danny Fox.

'They're not,' said the seal.

'Yes, they are,' said Danny Fox.

'No, they're not,' said the seal.

'Yes, they are,' said Danny Fox.

'No, they're not,' said the seal.

'Well,' said Danny Fox, 'the sea parrot is another name for puffin. I know that.'

'But the sea canary is the white whale,' said the seal.

'Tell him to line up,' said Danny Fox. 'He's long and big, I know.'

The seal called the white whale and told him to line up. Then he called the blue whale and the grey whale, the finback whale and the humpback whale, the beaked whale, the sperm whale, the finner whale, the pilot whale, the killer whale, the sharp-headed whale, the bow-headed whale and the square-headed grampus; and he told them to line up across the sea. Then he called the three kinds of sea pig – the dolphin, the porpoise, and the manatee. And then he called the walrus.

The walrus came puffing and blowing on to the beach, and when Danny saw his long yellow tusks and his fierce moustache, he put his tail between his legs and backed away growling, because he was afraid and trying not to show it.

'Put him in the very middle of the sea,' he told the seal. 'Next to the killer whale. And tell him if he feels someone walking over his back he's got to keep his mouth shut and stay still in the water, or the killer whale will bite him.'

'All right,' said the seal.

'Any more?' said Danny Fox.

'There's the turtles,' said the seal. 'Several kinds.'

'Turtles are reptiles,' said Danny Fox.

'There's the sea serpent,' said the seal.

'That's a reptile too,' said Danny. 'Reptiles don't count.'

'Well then,' said the seal, 'I can't think of anyone else – except the sea louse.'

'The sea louse!' said Danny Fox.

'Would you like to see him?' said the seal.

'Certainly not,' said Danny Fox. 'He's an insect and

insects don't count. And he sounds like an itchy insect and I wish you hadn't mentioned him because now I've got an itch.'

Danny Fox sat down and scratched behind his ear with his hind foot. Then he started biting his hind leg. Then he turned round and round on the rocky island, chasing his own tail.

'If you don't start counting soon,' said the seal, 'these animals will all swim away.'

'All right,' said Danny Fox.

'But how can you count them from here?' said the seal.

'Number one, that's you,' said Danny Fox. 'Keep swimming beside me while I count.'

And he walked over the back of the common seal and the fur seal and the harp seal and the hair seal and the golden seal, counting 'Two, three, four, five, six' in a loud voice. All the animals made a long bridge and he walked over the backs of sea lions, sea elephants, sea otters, sea wolves, and over the sea unicorn, until he reached the sea canary or white whale, counting all the time. And the seal was swimming beside him keeping count to see that he wasn't cheating. And when Danny Fox saw the long line of whales, lying in front of him on top of the water, nose to tail, he yelped with joy, because there were so many whales and their bodies were so long that he thought he would soon be home. And he scampered over the whales, forgetting his thinness and misery,

but suddenly one of them blew a spout of water and Danny Fox was shot up into the sky on top of the water spout and landed with a splash in the sea. The seal swam up to him quickly.

'Are you all right?' said the seal.

'Of course I am,' said Danny Fox. 'I got tired of counting and running, so I just jumped up in the air.'

'I see,' said the seal. 'Well luckily I kept count. You've got to number nine hundred and ninety-nine, and that's the killer whale. Swim after me. I'll show you where he is.'

Danny Fox swam after the seal and climbed on to the back of the killer whale.

'Tell him I shan't count him unless he keeps his mouth shut,' Danny Fox said.

'Keep your mouth shut, killer whale,' said the seal.

When he came to the end of the killer whale Danny Fox saw the long yellow tusks of the walrus, and then he saw something worse. He saw that the bridge of animals had come to an end. Far away in the distance the other seals were waiting, lined up near the shore.

'Did you say you'd brought some sea turtles?' said Danny Fox to the seal.

'Yes,' said the seal. 'But they are reptiles. You said they don't count.'

'I think I made a mistake,' said Danny. 'I think turtles ought to count as sea animals.'

But even when the seal brought the turtles and Danny

walked over them, counting, there was still a long way to go.

'Shall I call the sea louse?' said the seal.

'Certainly not, you stupid bearded seal,' said Danny crossly. He was trying to keep his balance on the last of the turtles which wobbled about in the water and had a slippery shell.

'But my dear Mr Phoca Barbata,' said Danny Fox, a minute later, 'did you mention a sea serpent, a little while ago?'

'I did,' said the seal. 'But he's a reptile too – he doesn't count.'

'Is he very long?' said Danny Fox.

'He's very long,' said the seal.

'Is he very sensitive?' said Danny Fox.

'He's very sensitive,' said the seal.

'And he's come all this way for nothing!!!'

'He's terribly annoyed,' said the seal.

'It's unfair on him, isn't it?' said Danny Fox.

'It's very unfair,' said the seal.

'Then don't you think you should call the sea serpent?' Danny Fox said.

'If you think it's all right,' said the seal.

'I don't like to be unfair,' said Danny Fox.

So the seal called the sea serpent and he was a mile long or more, and Danny Fox ran along him from his tail to his mouth and came to the marble seal and then to the monk seal and then to the elephant seal and then to the Atlantic grey seal and at last to the bottle-nosed seal, who had his front paws on the beach.

And Danny Fox scampered over the back of the bottle-nosed seal and ran up the sandy beach as fast as he could go.

7. The Fisherman Tricks Danny

Danny Fox was so hungry and tired after his long walk over the bridge of animals that he did not notice that he had landed on the beach just below the fisherman's house. He did not notice the fisherman's boat on the sands, nor his cart which was beside the house. And he walked very slowly up the beach, trying to think of a plan to get something to eat. The seal shouted after him, 'Now bring all the land animals here for me to count.'

'Oh, go away,' said Danny Fox.

The fisherman was sound asleep inside his house. He had been out fishing most of the night but had not caught any fish because the seals and dolphins and porpoises had chased them all away. And when the whales arrived in the early morning, he had started up his engine in a hurry and rushed home, afraid that they might upset his boat. So instead of driving to town to sell fish as usual, he had gone to the mill with his horse and cart to fetch some crushed oats. And when he came home from the mill and unloaded the sacks from the cart, he had spilt some of the oats on to the ground outside his door. Then he had gone to bed.

The fisherman had a cock and two hens. When the cock saw the oats on the ground he went 'cluck, cluck, cluck' to call the hens to the feast. He made such a loud noise that the duck and the goose and the hen who lived on the farm heard him too, and they all came running down to the fisherman's house to see what they could find to eat. And there they all were, pecking up oats in a greedy hurry, when Danny Fox arrived.

'Look out,' said the duck. 'There goes Danny Fox.'

'That's funny,' said the goose. 'He has swallowed a safety pin, and it's pinned the two sides of his tummy together and made him look thin.'

'That's not a safety pin,' said the hen.

'Yes, it is,' said the goose.

'No, it's not,' said the hen.

'What is it, then?' said the duck.

'It's just thinness,' said the hen. 'He's had nothing to eat for days and days and days, except one small fish for breakfast this morning.'

'How do you know?' said the duck.

'She doesn't,' said the goose.

'Yes, I do,' said the hen.

'No, you don't,' said the goose.

'Yes, I do,' said the hen. 'The sea robin told me this morning.'

And the fisherman's cock, who had said nothing all this time, suddenly shouted, 'Run away! Quick! And stop arguing.'

The fisherman's cock had seen Danny Fox just in time. Danny Fox had heard their voices and stood still. Then he had started stalking them, coming towards them very slowly, with his skinny nose stretched out in front and his poor threadbare tail stretched out behind him. And now the goose and the duck and the hens all ran away cackling and squawking, and the fisherman's cock flew up and perched on the side of the cart. Danny Fox began to chase the goose, which was the slowest, but he could not run very fast, he was so weak for want of food. And when he heard the cock crowing, he just sat down and gave up the chase.

'Danny Fox,' crowed the cock. 'You are old and thin. The goose says you've swallowed a safety pin.'

The fisherman's cock stood up on the side of the cart and ruffled his neck feathers and flapped his wings.

'If I am old,' said Danny Fox, 'that means I'm wiser. I've seen more things than you, and learned more lessons. And if I am thin, it's because I am always thinking out new clever tricks and I have no time to eat.'

'I can do some tricks too,' said the cock.

'Oh, can you?' said Danny Fox, coming nearer and nearer to the cart. He sat down just below the place where the cock was perching, and said, 'How many tricks can you do?'

'I can do three tricks,' said the cock, looking down at him out of one eye. 'How many tricks can you do?'

'Jump down here beside me and I'll show you,' Danny Fox said. The cock was very keen to learn a fourth trick, so he flew down from the cart and stood looking sideways at Danny Fox through the same eye. Birds can't look at things through both eyes at once, like a fox.

They tilt their heads sideways and see through one eye at a time.

'What tricks?' said the cock, with his head on one side.

'My grandfather used to shut one eye and give a great shout,' said Danny Fox.

'I could do that myself,' said the cock.

'I bet you can't shut the eye nearest me,' said Danny Fox. 'The one you are watching me with.'

'I bet I can,' said the cock.

'And give a great shout?' said Danny.

The cock shut his eye and squawked loudly, and he

could not see Danny Fox jumping at him. And Danny Fox caught him by the neck with his teeth and began to run away with him past the fisherman's window. And the cock squawked so loudly that the fisherman woke up and came running out of his house. And the fisherman's dog came running out of the other door and began to chase Danny Fox. And Danny Fox couldn't run very fast, but he could twist and turn more cleverly and quickly than the dog, and he went in circles and zigzags between the dog and the fisherman, who was dodging about trying to throw a piece of net over him and catch him. And gradually it got dark. But still Danny Fox held on to the cock. And the fisherman and his dog chased Danny Fox, with the cock squawking in his mouth, all night.

When morning came they were all exhausted. The fisherman was very angry. 'Let go of that cock, Danny Fox,' he called. 'That's my cock, Danny Fox.' He sang the words out as though they were part of a song.

'It sounds as if he's singing,' said the cock to Danny Fox, but Danny Fox did not answer.

'Let go, Danny Fox,' the fisherman sang.

'I'll tell you what to do, Danny Fox,' said the cock. 'Say, "Oh sweet-tongued singer, it is my own cock." When he hears that, he'll stop chasing you and he'll call his dog off.'

Danny Fox was very tired. He thought it best to do what the cock told him. He stood still for a moment and

79

called out to the fisherman, 'Oh sweet-tongued singer, it is my own cock!' And as he opened his mouth to say this, he dropped the cock and the cock sprang up to the roof of the fisherman's house and gave a loud crow.

The cock looked down at Danny Fox and said, 'I told you I could shut one eye and give a great shout.'

Danny Fox looked up at him scornfully but while he was curling his lips to show his fierce white teeth, the fisherman crept up behind him and the fisherman's dog came crouching along the ground in front and suddenly the fisherman threw his net over him and Danny Fox was caught.

As soon as he knew he could not escape from the net, Danny Fox lay still and allowed the fisherman to drag him into the house. He was too wise to struggle or fight. Instead, he began to think of a plan.

The fisherman picked him up in the net and let him drop into a wooden tub that stood beneath the window sill. Then he took the net away and nailed some boards across the top of the tub, like bars on top of a cage. The black tip of Danny Fox's nose could just get through, but no more, and he could only see out if he looked upwards towards the ceiling. He saw the fisherman's face looking down at him. The fisherman's dog and his cock and two hens and the goose and the duck and the hen from the farm all crowded into the house when they knew Danny Fox was a prisoner, and searched for crumbs on the floor.

'I knew I should catch you in the end,' the fisherman said.

'I think you like me very much,' said Danny Fox.

'Like you!' said the fisherman. 'How can I like you? You stole all my fish.'

'Then why did you want to catch me and keep me

near you? I think you do like me a bit,' said Danny Fox.

'How can you think that?' said the fisherman, looking down at him in the tub. 'When you made all the people in the town laugh at me.'

'I'm sorry they laughed at you,' said Danny Fox. 'But why did you want to catch me if you don't like me?'

'I am going to take you to the town,' the fisherman said, 'and I am going to show you to the people, so that they will believe what I told them.'

'What did you tell them?' said Danny Fox.

'I told them how I found a big dead fox on the road and threw him on to my cart.'

'That was true,' said Danny Fox. 'That was me.'

'And I told them how the fox came alive and stole all my fish.'

'And *that* was true,' said Danny Fox. 'I stole them with a very clever trick. And Mrs Doxie Fox and our three children Lick, Chew, and Swallow had a very good feed, thank you very much.'

'Well, the people would not believe me,' the fisherman said.

'What stupid people,' said Danny.

'All except the Princess,' the fisherman said.

'The Princess?' said Danny Fox, and held his head on one side.

'She was watching from her window,' the fisherman said. 'And she waved to show she believed me.'

'Are you going to take me to the town and show me to the Princess?' Danny Fox said.

'I shall show you to the people and she will watch from her window. She always watches me and my horse and cart when I am selling fish.'

'She likes me,' said Danny Fox.

'Who likes you?' said the fisherman.

'The Princess of course,' said Danny Fox. 'Do you like her?'

'Of course I do,' the fisherman said.

'Then if you like her, you must like me,' said Danny Fox.

'How can I like you, when you burnt all my clothes on the fire?' the fisherman said.

'But can't you see I had to?' Danny Fox said. 'And besides you've got better clothes now.'

'These are the farmer's clothes,' the fisherman said.

'Well you'd never have had such grand clothes if it hadn't been for me,' said Danny Fox. And the fisherman began to laugh because Danny Fox was so good at arguing.

8. The Fox in a Box

Then Danny Fox said to the fisherman, 'I hope you're not going to show me like this to the Princess and the people of the town?'

'Like what?' the fisherman said.

'When you first found me,' Danny Fox said, 'you spoke about my beautiful red coat and my beautiful thick red trousers. What will the townspeople think if they see me like this? I'm so worn and thin.'

'Yes, you look a bit rotten and mangy,' the fisherman said.

'And look at my beautiful long bushy tail. Half the hairs have fallen out!'

'Yes, it looks like an old toothbrush that someone has thrown away,' the fisherman said.

'Well, you can't let the Princess see me like this. You must give me lots to eat and let me run about, till I grow fat and glossy again.'

'I'll feed you,' said the fisherman, 'but I won't let you run about or you'll escape.'

But he hadn't caught any fish for two nights and he was so poor that all he could find to give to Danny were some old potato peelings and a hard stale crust.

When night time came the fisherman went out in his boat. 'Tomorrow, I'll take you to town with my horse and cart,' he said to Danny Fox.

He left the dog on guard. 'You watch Danny Fox doesn't bite his way out through the bars,' he said to his dog.

As soon as Danny Fox heard the engine of the motor boat fading away out to sea he began to bark and howl inside the tub.

'Be quiet,' said the dog. 'What's the matter with you?'

'I'm hungry,' Danny Fox said.

'So am I,' said the dog. 'I only had potato skins and a crust of bread for dinner. But I'm not making a fuss.'

'A crust of bread!' said Danny Fox. 'That's funny. Your master gave me a huge big meal.'

'He didn't!' said the dog.

'Yes, he did,' said Danny Fox.

'No, he didn't,' said the dog.

'Yes, he did,' said Danny Fox.

'No, he didn't,' said the dog.

'Yes, he did,' said Danny Fox. 'He gave me a whole chicken all to myself, and a big piece of salmon, and a hunk of cheese as thick as your head.'

'He didn't,' said the dog. 'I would have smelt it.'

'You were out at my dinner time,' said Danny Fox.

'But when I came home, all I could smell was old potato peelings and stale bread,' said the dog.

'That's because I ate up every scrap of it,' said Danny Fox. 'I ate the chicken, bones and all.'

The dog put his front paws on top of the tub and looked down through the bars at Danny Fox.

'Did you really have chicken?' he said.

'Of course I did,' said Danny Fox.

'I love chicken,' said the dog. 'And now I hate my master for giving you all that, when I had potato skins and a stale crust.'

'He's promised me chicken and cheese for breakfast,' Danny Fox said. 'And fish too, if he catches some to-night.'

'But why?' said the dog, and growled with rage.

'Because he wants me to look fat and sleek when he shows me off in town tomorrow,' said Danny Fox.

The dog growled angrily. 'He never takes me to town,' he said. 'I have to guard the house.'

'Would you like me to give you my breakfast?' Danny Fox said.

'You couldn't,' said the dog. 'My master would see.'

'He cuts it up and pushes it through the bars,' said Danny Fox. 'If you were lying down inside this tub, you'd get it and he'd never know. And he would take you to town after breakfast.'

The dog felt hungrier and hungrier as he listened to Danny Fox.

'How would I get into the tub?' he said.

'Can't you pull out the nails with your teeth?' said Danny Fox. 'And loosen a couple of bars?'

The dog pulled at the nails and they came out easily.

Danny Fox pushed the bars aside with his nose and jumped out.

'Now in you get,' he said to the dog, and the dog jumped into the tub.

'Luckily the tip of your nose is black like mine,' said Danny Fox. 'If you lie down till your breakfast comes the fisherman will think you are me.'

'Oh thank you,' said the dog. 'You are kind.'

Danny Fox pushed the bars back into position. He tried to nail them down again, but of course he couldn't.

'Remember to lie quite still,' he said to the dog. 'Don't move or make a noise, whatever happens.' And Danny Fox ran away and left him there.

The fisherman came home in the early morning, just as it was beginning to get light. But inside his house it was still rather dark. He could not see very much. But he did notice that two of the bars had come loose. He peered into the tub to make sure that the fox was still there, and when he saw a black nose in the shadowy darkness, he said to himself, 'That's all right, he's asleep.' Then he fetched his hammer and made the bars firm again. Then he covered the tub with a sack and carried it out to his cart.

He loaded the cart with boxes of fish. And he took a large, old fishing net with him as well.

He had caught plenty of fish that night and he set out for the town, happily thinking, 'First I'll sell my fish. And then I'll take the sack off the tub and let the people see what a big fox I've caught.'

Danny Fox had been hiding outside the back door all this time, waiting to see what would happen. When he saw the fisherman start off for the town, he ran by a short cut across the fields, as fast as he could go. The horse and cart was slow and Danny Fox was quick and Danny Fox arrived at the market place in the middle of the town in the early morning before any of the people were awake. He was looking for a good place to hide in and watch what would happen when the fisherman discovered the dog in the tub.

Suddenly he heard a voice that seemed to come from the sky.

It was the Princess calling to him from her bedroom window in the Palace.

'Good morning, Mr Fox,' she said.

Danny looked up and saw her with her elbows on the window sill, watching him.

'Hullo, Princess,' said Danny Fox. 'If I come up and see you, will you let me wear your crown again?'

'Yes, if you promise not to play any tricks,' said the Princess. She came down to open the door and Danny Fox dived past her in such a hurry to run upstairs that he nearly knocked her over.

From the Princess's window they had a fine view of the square. They could see the people drawing their bedroom curtains in the houses opposite, and opening the shutters of the shop windows. They could see six sleepy cows wandering through the square on their way to a field, for the town was small and old fashioned and the milkman kept his cows in a shed at the back of his shop. And at last they saw the fisherman's cart coming slowly round the corner and they heard him shout, 'Come buy my fresh fish. Fresh mackerel and herring. Come buy my fresh fish, caught early this morning.'

He made his horse stop in the middle of the market square and he looked up for a second at the Princess's window. She waved to him, and Danny Fox hid behind her just in time. And then the people all came running out of their houses with dishes and pans for the fish and money for the fisherman. And when they saw the big boxes of fish on the cart, they said, 'Oh he's got some lovely fish today!' And then they saw the tub with the sack over it, and they said, 'I wonder what he's got in that tub?'

The fisherman stood up proudly on his cart.

'I'll tell you what I've got in my tub,' he said.

'What can it be?' said the people.

'It is the fox that stole my fish the other day,' said the fisherman. 'You didn't believe me when I said I'd found a large dead fox lying in the road.'

'And is he dead?' said the people.

'He was dead,' said the fisherman. 'But he came alive and stole my fish and now I have caught him again.'

And all the people shouted, 'Show him to us! Show him to us!'

But the fisherman would not take the sack off the tub until he had sold his fish. While the people were buying fish, Danny Fox was rushing round and round the Princess's room, crashing against the bed and chairs and bumping into the Princess's legs because he was so excited he didn't know what he was doing. Every now and then he put his paws up on the window sill and looked down at the tub in the cart, wagging his tail.

'Why are you so pleased?' the Princess said. 'Is the fox in the tub a particular friend of yours?' Danny Fox didn't answer. He went on wagging his tail.

When the fisherman had sold all his fish, the Princess pulled her chair nearer to the window and put her elbows on the window sill and her chin in her hands, and looked down to see what was happening. Danny Fox was beside her standing on his hind legs, with his paws on the

window sill looking out. But he was ready to hide whenever he thought the fisherman might look up.

The fisherman piled up the empty fish boxes and lifted the tub on top of them. And all the people in the market

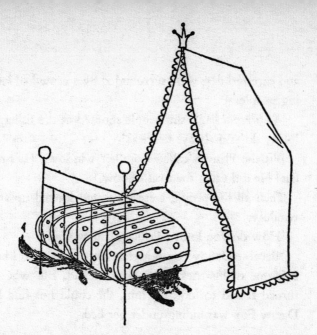

square were watching him, very excited because they wanted to see the big red fox. He fixed the fishing net round the cart on poles to make a cage. Then he took the bars off the tub.

'Come on, Danny Fox! Jump out of the tub!' the fisherman said.

The old dog was tired of waiting in the dark for a grand breakfast that never arrived and when he heard his master's voice he jumped out, barking and looking dazed and stupid.

When the people saw an ordinary old black and white dog, instead of a big red fox, they began to laugh, and other people came running into the square to see what they were laughing at until the fisherman and his horse and cart and dog were surrounded by a crowd of laughing people.

'You are a liar!' the people shouted at the fisherman. 'Why do you always tell lies?'

But the Princess called from her window, 'He's not a liar! He did catch the fox! I know.'

Then all the people were quiet and looked up at her window.

'How do you know, Princess?' they said.

'Because Danny Fox is here in my room. And I know it is one of his tricks,' the Princess said. But when she turned round to look for him, she could not find him. Danny Fox was hiding under her bed.

9. Danny Helps the Princess

The fisherman called to the Princess. 'May I come into your palace and catch the fox again?' he said.

But the Princess made signs to show it was too dangerous. She thought the Queen might find him in the palace and lock him up in prison.

'I'll try to catch him for you,' she said. 'I think he's in the cupboard, or under the bed.'

Then she heard Danny Fox whimpering under the bed. Then she saw his nose sticking out.

'Yes, there he is,' she said, 'I'll throw him out of the window. He won't hurt himself if you catch him in the net.'

'Please don't throw me out,' said Danny Fox.

'Why not? You tricked him, didn't you?' the Princess said.

Then Danny Fox came up to her and licked her hand. He told her how he had tempted the dog and made him get into the tub. The Princess wanted to be cross with him but she could not stop herself laughing.

'I am clever, aren't I?' Danny Fox said.

The Princess tried not to laugh.

'If you let me go, and don't throw me down,' said Danny Fox, 'I'll make your best wish come true.'

'What do you mean?' the Princess said.

'What would you like best in all the world?' said Danny Fox.

'That's a secret,' the Princess said.

'If you tell me the secret, I can make it come true,' said Danny Fox.

The Princess knelt on the floor beside him and whispered in his ear.

'I want to marry the fisherman,' she said. And then she sneezed because Danny Fox's furry ear tickled her nose.

'That's simple,' said Danny Fox. 'I'll fix it up for you.'

'You couldn't do that,' the Princess said. 'My stepmother, the Queen, won't allow it.'

'Is your stepmother clever at tricks?' said Danny Fox.

'No, she's stupid and horrid,' the Princess said. 'She wants me to marry a very rich man.'

'Why doesn't she like the fisherman?' said Danny Fox.

'Because he is poor,' said the Princess.

'Then I know how to make her like him,' said Danny Fox.

'How?' said the Princess.

'If you let me go free, I'll show you,' Danny Fox said.

The Princess believed him, but before she let him go she picked him up in her arms and showed him to all the

97

people in the square. She told them how the fisherman had caught him and how he had escaped by a trick. Then she made a secret sign to the fisherman and he knew he must go home. The secret sign meant that the Queen, her stepmother, had come into the room.

When the Queen saw Danny Fox in the Princess's arms, she was cross.

'Put that nasty thing down,' she said. But Danny Fox whispered in the Princess's ear, 'Tell her I'm worth a hundred million pounds.'

'But are you?' said the Princess, whispering.

'Well, Doxie would rather have me than a hundred million pounds, so I must be worth that.'

'I see,' the Princess whispered. Then she said aloud, 'This fox is worth a hundred million pounds.'

'Then how did you get hold of it?' said the Queen.

'Tell her a rich man gave me to you,' whispered Danny Fox.

'I can't say that. It isn't true!' the Princess said.

When Danny Fox saw that the Princess would not tell a lie, he jumped out of her arms and walked up to the Queen.

'I am the best fox in the world,' he said, 'and my master is the richest man in the world. He caught me and gave me to the Princess.'

'Is this true?' said the Queen.

The Princess shook her head.

'The man who caught me wants to marry her,' said Danny Fox.

'Is that true?' said the Queen.

'Yes, it's true,' the Princess said.

And Danny Fox said, 'He came to see her early this morning. She opened the door, but wouldn't let him in.'

'Oh, please don't tell lies,' the Princess said.

'It's you who are telling lies,' screamed the Queen, growing red in the face with anger. 'I heard you go downstairs this morning early. Tell me where the rich man lives, you stupid girl. We must send for him at once.'

'I don't know any rich men,' said the Princess.

The Queen's hair stood up on end like a porcupine's quills and she rushed away to fetch the King. She told him to come at once and give the Princess a smacking.

'What for?' said the King, who did not like smacking people.

'Because she's pretending not to know where a rich man lives,' said the Queen. 'She can't think of anything except that dirty young fisherman.'

When the King came, the Princess was sitting by the window with Danny Fox on her lap.

'Now,' said the King. 'Please tell the Queen where

the rich man lives. Or else she'll make me smack you.'

The Princess said, 'I don't know any rich men. Oh please don't smack me!' And she began to cry. 'Oh, I wish my fisherman was here,' she sobbed.

'Do you hear that!' screamed the Queen. 'Now smack her.' Her voice was like the sound of somebody smashing a plate on the floor.

Danny Fox jumped down from the Princess's lap and walked across the room very proudly, and showed the King and Queen his fierce white teeth. The King and Queen were frightened.

'I know where the rich man lives,' said Danny Fox. 'I can bring him here if you like. But first you must make two promises.'

'Oh dear,' said the Queen. 'Do you think he will bite?'

'I won't bite if you promise not to smack the Princess,'

said Danny Fox. 'And I'll fetch the rich man if you give me a big breakfast now, and a big dinner when I come back with him.'

The King and Queen promised. They gave Danny Fox a great big breakfast and, when he had eaten it, he ran off by his short cut through the fields as quick as he could go, and jumped over a wall into the road right in front of the fisherman's cart.

The fisherman's dog ran up to him growling. The hair on the dog's back stood on end and he held his tail up stiffly.

'You cheated me,' he said, 'And I can see by your big fat tummy that you've had a big fat breakfast.'

'Yes,' said Danny Fox. 'As a matter of fact I had breakfast at the Palace, with the Queen.'

'I'll tear you to bits,' said the dog.

'No, don't,' said Danny Fox. 'Or you won't get any dinner. But if you do what I tell you, the Queen will give you the biggest dinner you've ever had in your life.'

'I don't believe you,' said the dog. 'But I'm hungry.'

'Then go and fetch a hundred other dogs and tell them to sit outside the palace, in the market square,' said Danny Fox.

'Do you promise they'll all get dinner?' said the dog.

'They'll all get dinner,' Danny Fox said.

'I don't believe you,' said the dog. 'But I'll bring a hundred dogs and if the Queen doesn't give us any dinner, we'll tear you to bits.'

The fisherman's dog ran off and the fisherman shook his whip at Danny Fox.

'You must come back with me to the Palace,' said Danny Fox to him. 'The King and Queen want to see you.'

At first the fisherman would not go. He thought it was another trick, but Danny Fox stood on his hind legs, resting his front paws on the shaft of the cart, and told him why the Princess had let him go. 'I can make the Queen like you,' Danny Fox said. 'I can make the Queen order you to marry the Princess.'

'How could you?' said the fisherman.

'Because the Queen can't see real people,' said Danny Fox. 'She can only see whether a man is rich or poor.'

'She'll see my old clothes,' the fisherman said. 'And she'll know I am poor, because I've been working hard, and even the good clothes the farmer gave me have plenty of holes in them now.'

'She won't see your clothes,' said Danny, and when they came to a muddy pond outside the town he told the fisherman to stop and stand up on the edge of the cart.

When the fisherman stood up, Danny Fox suddenly bumped into him and knocked him head over heels into the slushy mud.

'So it was another trick!' said the fisherman, angrily, trying to get the mud out of his eyes and nose and mouth. 'And my clothes are much worse now! How can I go and see the Queen all covered in mud?'

But Danny Fox said, 'Don't worry, leave your horse and cart here and follow me.'

When they got to the market square he told the fisherman to hide behind some empty orange boxes. Then he went to the Queen and said that the rich man had had a terrible accident.

'He fell into the pond,' said Danny Fox. 'His clothes are ruined, and he says he can't come and see you.'

'Oh don't let him go,' the Queen screamed. 'Lend him your best suit, will you King!'

'All right,' said the King. 'Princess. Take it out to him will you?'

'Be quick,' said the Queen.

Danny Fox and the Princess found a tub of rain water in an old garden which was hidden from the windows of the palace and there the fisherman washed the mud away and dressed himself in the King's best suit of cloth of gold with precious jewels for buttons.

There were many trees in the garden and, as it was nearly Christmas time, their brown and golden leaves were lying on the ground. There had been no rain for weeks. The leaves were dry and rustly. They made a lovely sound when the Princess and the fisherman walked through them, or when Danny Fox pushed them up with his nose and made them fly in the air.

'Make a big heap of leaves,' said Danny Fox. 'I am going back to see the Queen.'

'All the rich man's money bags are spoiled with mud,' said Danny Fox to the Queen. 'Can you lend him a big sack to keep his money in?'

The Queen fetched the biggest sack she could find. It was far bigger than a coal-sack. Danny Fox took one end

of it in his mouth and dragged it back to the garden. He told the fisherman and the Princess to fill it up with leaves. And then he went back to the Queen. He saw the fisherman's dog arriving with a hundred friends, who all sat down in the market square and gazed hungrily at the Palace.

'Oh dear,' said the Queen. 'Look at all those dogs outside my Palace. The market square is full of dogs. What can it mean?'

'Those are just a few of the rich man's watchdogs,' Danny Fox said. 'He brings those with him wherever he goes, to guard his pocket money.'

'A hundred dogs to guard his pocket money!' said the Queen. 'I've just been counting them.'

'A hundred and one,' said Danny Fox. 'And by the way, that sack wasn't nearly big enough to hold his pocket money. Please give me some more.'

The Queen gave him six more, and while the fisherman filled the empty ones with leaves, Danny Fox dragged the full ones into the square and told the dogs to sit round them in a circle.

And every few minutes, Danny Fox ran back to the Queen to ask for more sacks, until at last there was a huge pile of bulging sacks in the middle of the market square. If any one had climbed to the top of it, he would have been able to look in at the Princess's window.

'I don't believe those sacks are full of money!' said the Queen. 'It looks like waste paper to me.'

'They are full of ten-pound notes. Go and look,' said Danny Fox.

'I'm frightened of the dogs,' said the Queen.

And Danny Fox said, 'The rich man wouldn't need a hundred watchdogs if the sacks were full of waste paper, would he?'

'That's true,' said the Queen. 'Please ask him to come and see me quickly.'

'I'll try,' said Danny Fox. 'But he's shy about his clothes. He's a bit ashamed of the suit the King lent him.'

'Ashamed of it!' said the King. 'It's my best suit.'

'He's used to much better clothes than yours,' said Danny Fox. Then he went and fetched the fisherman.

The Queen did not know it was the fisherman of course. She never looked at people's faces, only at their clothes. She made a very low curtsy and brought him into the palace. She showed him a chair made of silver.

'Please sit down,' said the Queen.

The fisherman was afraid he might spoil the silver chair and he would not sit down.

'He doesn't like cheap old chairs, like that,' said Danny Fox.

'Oh dear,' said the Queen. 'It's the best chair we've got. It cost a hundred pounds.'

'Never mind,' said Danny Fox. 'But perhaps you could bring a better table.'

'That table's made of gold,' said the Queen. 'Oh dear, why is he staring at it so?'

The fisherman was staring because he had never seen a golden table in all his life before. But Danny Fox said, 'He's a bit shocked to see a golden table here in your best room. In his house the back doorstep is made of gold. The chairs and tables are made of lovely stuff which you have never seen.'

'Oh dear,' said the Queen, 'I'm so sorry.'

'Oh, my dear sir,' she said to the fisherman, 'I'm afraid we've got nothing that's good enough for you.'

'You've only got one thing,' the fisherman said.

'Oh tell me what it is and I'll give it to you,' said the Queen.

'It is the Princess,' the fisherman said.

'Do you want her as a slave?' said the Queen.

'I want to marry her,' the fisherman said.

'She is a naughty girl,' said the Queen. 'She says she wants to marry a poor fisherman.'

'Speak to her crossly,' Danny Fox said.

Then the Queen's hair stood on end like a porcupine's quills and her face was red. And she screamed at the Princess in a voice like somebody smashing a plate on the floor.

'You must marry this man!' screamed the Queen.

And of course the Princess said, 'Yes, I will.'

Then they all took hands and made a ring round Danny Fox and danced for joy. And Danny Fox turned round and round in the middle of the ring chasing his tail. And when they were tired of dancing, and he was tired of chasing his tail, they had a big feast and Danny Fox asked the Queen to send the biggest feast of all out to the fisherman's dog and his hundred friends who were waiting in the market square. And Danny Fox and the fisherman's dog and the hundred other dogs ate till their tummies bulged like footballs and they could hardly move. And while the Queen was greedily eating an ice-cream filled with cherries and almonds, the size of a rich man's hat, the fisherman fetched his horse and cart secretly and took away the sacks of pretending money. And he promised to come back next day and marry the Princess. And all the dogs went away. And at last Danny

Fox stretched his legs – first, his front legs, then his hind legs – and he said, 'Now I must go home to my den, which is a good cave on the side of the mountain. I must go home, because I am lonely for Mrs Doxie Fox and for our three children, Lick, Chew, and Swallow.'

10. Danny Fox Goes Home

The Princess came with Danny Fox to the door of the Palace, to say 'Good-bye'. She opened a chest beside the front door and began to sort out a pile of sacks made of fine silk in every colour of the rainbow. She filled five silken sacks with food for him to take home – a red sack full of food for Danny, a yellow one for Mrs Doxie Fox, a green one for Lick, a blue one for Chew, and a violet one for Swallow. Then she filled five other sacks with sumptuous wedding cake, with white icing and pink icing, and 'hundreds and thousands' of every bright colour – one sackful for Lick, one for Chew, one for Swallow, one for Mrs Doxie Fox, and one for Danny.

'How on earth will you carry them all?' the Princess said to Danny.

'I'll take the biggest one in my mouth,' said Danny Fox. 'Please tie the others on to me.'

So the Princess tied three silken sacks round his chest, a red one on his back and yellow ones against his ribs on each side. And then she tied three round his middle – another red one on his back, and two green ones against his tummy. And then she tied three to his tail – a blue one at the top, a violet one on its bushy middle part and another blue one at its beautiful white tip.

'And now,' said the Princess, 'you look like a prince in a coat of many colours, but I think that's too big a load for you to carry up the mountain.'

'I've shown you how clever I am,' said Danny Fox. 'And now I can show you how strong I am.'

'All right,' said the Princess. 'But wait a minute. I haven't given you your special present yet.'

'What can that be?' said Danny Fox. He couldn't wag his tail because the silken sacks were too heavy.

The Princess went away and came back holding her crown.

'This is for you,' she said, and put it over his head. 'You'll have to wear it like a necklace, as before, because your head is too small.'

Danny Fox was terribly pleased. 'Do I REALLY look like a Prince?' he said. And the Princess bent down and kissed his furry red forehead.

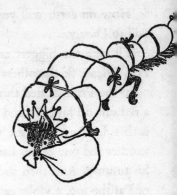

'Yes, like a Prince,' she said.

'That's right,' said Danny Fox. 'That's what I am. Thank you. Good-bye.'

'Good-bye!' the Princess shouted after him as he went lollopy-loping away from her, across the market square and out into the country. She ran upstairs to the topmost tower of the palace and watched him going homewards by his short cut. From there he looked like a tiny speck of coloured light crossing the green fields. The Princess was sad because he had gone. She put her hands up to her mouth and shouted, 'Come back, one day!' But Danny Fox was too far away to hear her.

Danny Fox could not go fast because the presents were heavy. When he came to the farm at the foot of the mountain, he longed to have a rest, but he was afraid to sit down because he knew that if the farmer saw him he would not be able to run away quickly.

He limped, lollopy-lollop, past the farm, and the duck and the goose and the hen were watching him.

'Look out,' said the duck. 'There goes Danny Fox!'

'That's funny,' said the goose. 'He's grown golden fur on his neck, and the fur on his body and tail is coloured like a rainbow.'

'That's not fur,' said the hen.

'Yes, it is,' said the goose.

'No, it's not,' said the hen.

'What is it, then?' said the duck.

'The gold on his neck is a golden crown, which he is wearing like a necklace,' said the hen. 'And the bright colours round his body and tail are silken sacks full of presents.'

Danny Fox went lolloping past the mouse's hole.

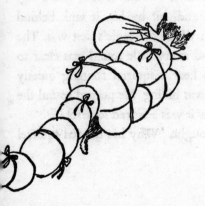

'That's funny,' said the mouse. 'I can see a rainbow walking along, but it's got legs like a fox.'

'Rainbows don't have legs,' said the pigeon who was flying up above.

'Yes, they do,' said the mouse.

'No, they don't,' said the pigeon.

'This one does,' said the mouse.

The silken sacks grew heavier and heavier as Danny Fox climbed the mountain, and when he came near his cave he hid behind a large boulder and lay down to rest. He would have been more comfortable if he had gone a few steps further, into the warm darkness of his den. But he was too proud to let his family know that he felt tired. He wanted to get his breath back, and then jump up and run home with the presents, pretending he had galloped all the way up the hill. But even when he was tired, he always watched everything and listened to every sound.

It was late in the evening now. The frost had begun to make patterns like white lace on black twigs of heather and brown leaves of bracken. The sun looked like a big, orange-coloured penny and, bit by bit, it sank behind the top of the mountain where the eagle's nest was. The air was cold and still and every little sound was clear to Danny. He could even hear a squirrel running quietly past the rock where he was hiding. He peeped round the edge of the rock and saw it was a fat red squirrel.

'That's funny,' he thought. 'Why has the red squirrel

left his woods and climbed all the way up the mountain?'

Danny Fox listened and he heard Lick's voice.

'You can't come in,' said Lick to the red squirrel.

'Is your mother not at home?' said the red squirrel.

Then Danny Fox heard Lick say, 'Yes, she's at home, but she's crying in a corner because she thinks our Daddy is drowned and dead.'

'What happened to your Daddy?' said the squirrel.

'An eagle carried him over the sea and dropped him.'

'Then he must be dead,' said the red squirrel.

When Danny Fox heard that he growled to show he was alive, but the squirrel did not hear him, and went on talking. 'Tell your mother I've brought her some beautiful nuts,' he said. 'Tell her I'll comfort her and bring her nuts every day.'

Then Danny heard Lick shouting to Mrs Doxie Fox who was inside the cave. Lick shouted, 'There's a person here who says he'll comfort you and bring you nuts every day.'

'There's only one person who can comfort me,' Mrs Doxie Fox called out, 'and he wears a beautiful red coat.'

'Well, this person's wearing a red coat,' said Lick.

'Is he wearing beautiful thick red trousers?' said Mrs Doxie Fox.

'Yes,' said Lick.

'Has he got a beautiful long bushy tail?' said Mrs Doxie Fox.

'Yes,' said Lick. 'Shall I let him in?'

Before Mrs Doxie Fox could answer Danny shouted 'NO!' and leapt out from behind the boulder where he had been hiding. Lick and the red squirrel were frightened and they both ran away.

The squirrel saw his foxy face and ran down the mountain. Lick saw ten rainbow-coloured sacks come flying at him through the air, and he heard a fierce growling. He ran into the cave and hid behind his mother. Chew and Swallow heard the growls and hid there too. Even Swallow did not recognize his Daddy's voice. And Danny Fox decided to play a trick on them.

He lay down outside the cave and hid his nose in a

clump of heather. Then he put on a strange deep voice and said, 'Is Mrs Doxie Fox at home?'

'Come on,' said Lick. 'We must be brave.' And Lick, Chew, and Swallow went as near to the entrance of the cave as they dared.

'Yes, she's at home,' said Lick, 'but she's crying in a corner because our Daddy is drowned and dead.'

'You can't come in,' said Chew.

'We'll bite you if you do,' said Swallow.

'Tell her I've brought her some sumptuous wedding cake,' said Danny Fox in his funny deep voice. 'And lots of other things to eat. And tell her to let me in because I want to comfort her.'

Lick, Chew, and Swallow told their mother what he said.

'Is he wearing a red coat?' said Mrs Doxie Fox.

Lick very bravely looked under the rainbow-coloured silken sacks and said, 'Yes.'

'Is he wearing beautiful thick red trousers?' said Mrs Doxie Fox.

Chew very bravely looked under more rainbow-coloured silken sacks and said, 'Yes.'

'Has he got a beautiful long smooth nose with a beautiful black tip?' said Mrs Doxie Fox.

'His nose is hidden in a clump of heather,' they all said, and the nose growled, pretending to be fierce.

'Please look at it!' called Mrs Doxie Fox.

'It's your turn,' said Chew to Lick.

'No, it's your turn,' said Lick to Chew.

'I'll look,' said Swallow, who wasn't a bit afraid.

It was nearly dark now and though Swallow pushed his nose bravely into the clump of heather he could not see very much. But, for foxes, smelling is better than seeing, and he smelt Danny Fox and he knew there was no one else in the world who smelt like that, and he wagged his tail. And Danny Fox whispered to him, 'Yes, it is me. But let's go on pretending.'

So Swallow shouted out, 'Yes, he has got a beautiful long smooth nose with a beautiful black tip!'

'Has he got a beautiful long bushy tail with a beautiful white tip?' said Mrs Doxie Fox.

'Bite the silk thread,' whispered Danny Fox to Swallow. 'And pull the sacks away. And then you will all see my tail.'

Swallow bit the thread off in such a hurry that he swallowed it. And Lick, Chew, and Swallow looked closely at Danny Fox's tail.

'OH YES!' they shouted to Mrs Doxie Fox. 'He's got the most beautiful long bushy white-tipped tail we've ever seen!'

And when Mrs Doxie Fox heard that, she jumped up from her sad corner and came running to the entrance of the cave just before the sun went down behind the mountain. And she was in time to see Danny Fox pull his head out of the clump of heather. And she licked his

lovely face all over and she looked at the golden crown on his neck. And Danny licked her face and they both licked the faces of Lick, Chew, and Swallow and they – especially Lick – licked back. And they all wagged their tails and clambered over one another, tugging at the silken threads and opening the rainbow-coloured silken sacks.

And they all had the biggest feast they had ever eaten in all their lives. And when they had finished eating, the sun had disappeared behind the mountain and the mountainside was dark and very cold. So they went into their cave and cuddled together to keep warm. And they looked like a big furry bundle, but nobody saw what they looked like because they were asleep in a safe place.

And there was so much food left over that Danny Fox didn't have to go out hunting or searching for a very long time.

Some other Young Puffins

THE BUREAUCATS
Richard Adams

Imagine events in a large household, seen through the eyes of Richard and Thomas Kitten, who feel life should be organized entirely around them – it isn't, of course, and the consequences are highly entertaining.

THE RAILWAY CAT AND DIGBY
Phyllis Arkle

Further adventures of Alfie, the railway cat, who always seems to be in Leading Railman Hack's bad books. Alfie is a lot smarter than many people think, and he would like to be friends with Hack. But when he tries to improve matters by 'helping' Hack's dog, Digby, win a prize at the local show, the situation rapidly goes from bad to worse!

RAT SATURDAY
Margaret Nash

Does 'Old Teabag' really live in a damp cellar with rats running up his legs? Joe doesn't believe it, but all the same, he decides to find out. Imagine his surprise when he meets two very friendly, very tame pet rats! It's not long before Joe and his friend Donna discover that tame rats can be a lot of fun.

THE PICTURE PRIZE AND OTHER STORIES FOR THE VERY YOUNG
Simon Watson

A picture competition in which Wallace gets paint in some very unusual places, an escaped horse which has to be taken home, magic chickens and great, hairy, striped caterpillars – these are just a few of the exciting things that come into Wallace's life.

TALES FROM ALLOTMENT LANE SCHOOL
Margaret Joy

Twelve delightful stories, bright, light and funny, about the children in Miss Mee's class at Allotment Lane School. Meet Ian, the avid collector; meet Mary and Gary, who have busy mornings taking messages; and meet the school caterpillars, who disappear and turn up again in surprising circumstances. Get to know Miss Mee and her class and you will wish you could go to Allotment Lane School too.

DUCK BOY
Christobel Mattingley

The holiday at Mrs Perry's farm doesn't start very well for Adam. His elder brother and sister don't want to spend any time with him; *they* say he's too young. At first he's bored and lonely, but then he discovers the creek and meets two old ducks who obviously need some help. Every year their eggs are stolen by rats or foxes, so Adam strikes a bargain with them: he'll help guard their nest, if they'll let him learn to swim in their creek.

RAGDOLLY ANNA
THREE CHEERS FOR RAGDOLLY ANNA
Jean Kenward

Although she's only made from a morsel of this and a tatter of that, Ragdolly Anna is a very special doll. And within hours of beginning to live with the Little Dressmaker, the White Cat and Dummy, she embarks on some hair-raising adventures. (Featured on ITV.)

THE PERFECT HAMBURGER
Alexander McCall Smith

If only Joe could remember *exactly* what he had thrown so haphazardly into the mixing bowl, he knew that his perfect hamburger could revive his friend Mr Borthwick's ailing business and drive every other fast-food store off the high street. A grand opening announcing the perfect hamburger is arranged – but will Joe and Mr Borthwick find the vital ingredient in time?

THE THREE AND MANY WISHES OF JASON REID
Hazel Hutchins

Eleven-year-old Jason is a very good thinker. So when Quicksilver (no more than eighteen inches high) grants him three wishes, he's extremely wary. After all, in fairy tales this kind of thing always leads to disaster. So Jason is absolutely determined to get *his* wishes right. But it's not that easy, and he lands himself and his friends in all sorts of terrible but funny scrapes!

MR BERRY'S ICE-CREAM PARLOUR
Jennifer Zabel

It is thrilling enough to have a lodger in the house – after all, not even Andrew Brimblecombe has a lodger – but Carl is over the moon when he discovers that Mr Berry plans to open an ice-cream parlour.